⚞ ONCE UPON A WORLD ⚟

THE GLASS PALACE

An Arabian Fairy Tale

and also
SLEEPING BEAUTY

by **SAVIOUR PIROTTA**
and **ALAN MARKS**

W
FRANKLIN WATTS
LONDON•SYDNEY

First published in 2004
by Franklin Watts
96 Leonard Street
London EC2A 4XD

Franklin Watts Australia
45-51 Huntley Street
Alexandria
NSW 2015

Text copyright © Saviour Pirotta 2004
Illustrations copyright © Alan Marks 2004

Editor: Rachel Cooke
Series design: Jonathan Hair

A CIP catalogue record for this book is available
from the British Library

ISBN: 0 7496 5433 3 (hbk)
        0 7496 5789 8 (pbk)

Printed in Singapore

Contents

 # *Once upon a time*

Sleeping Beauty is one of the most popular stories in the world and different versions of it can be found in many countries. In Europe, it was first made popular around 1636 by the Italian writer Gianbattista Basile. His tale was a big influence on the French writer Perrault and the German brothers Grimm who wrote their own versions. These two are now the most well-known.

Both these versions, and others told around the world, are full of symbols – images and events with hidden meanings. They are really about growing up, focusing on the scary process of changing from a child to an adult.

In *Sleeping Beauty*, retold at the end of this book from the tale by the brothers Grimm, the witch's curse is a symbol of the danger and pain that

lurk through an adult's life. The king destroying all the spinning wheels in the land shows parents' attempts to shelter their children from the dangers of this world. But they cannot do this for ever. Inevitably, the princess finds the one spinning wheel left in the country. The story ends with a positive message: the princess survives the one hundred years and wakes up safe and sound – a grown-up ready to face her new life.

See if you can find any of these symbols in *The Glass Palace*. This story is from the Middle East and was first published as *The Ninth Captain's Tale* in *The Book of 1001 Nights*. Readers of *Sleeping Beauty* sometimes complain that the princess does nothing to stop what happens to her. The same cannot be said of Sittukhan, the heroine of *The Glass Palace*. Read it and see how she deals with the injustices that life throws at her.

The Glass Palace

In a distant city of golden minarets, there once lived a young merchant's wife who very much wanted a child. She had been married for several years, but as hard as she wished, the cradle by her bed remained empty. Her friends gave her pitying looks and her mother-in-law complained loudly at every opportunity: 'When will I have a grandchild?' In desperation, the young woman went to see a powerful witch.

'Give me three bags of gold,' said the enchantress, 'and I'll give you a daughter as dazzling as the summer dawn.'

'Alas,' cried the merchant's wife, 'I do not have three bags of gold.'

'Give me two, then,' snapped the old woman. 'Your girl will not be perfect for such a price but men will find her as enchanting as a nightingale.'

'Alas,' said the merchant's wife, 'I do not have two bags of gold either.'

'Then give me one bag,' cried the witch. 'And the child shall only be pretty.'

'But I have only a handful of coins,' sobbed the merchant's wife.

'For that,' sneered the greedy enchantress, 'your daughter shall be truly beautiful. But she will have one small problem! If she so much as touches a piece of cotton, she will fall down dead.'

The young woman had no choice. She paid the coins and left, praying the witch would keep her word.

And so it seemed she did. Nine months later the merchant's wife gave birth to a girl, whom she called Sittukhan. She wrapped the child in linen and she and her husband made sure that not a scrap of cotton ever entered the house.

Their daughter grew up to be as beautiful and graceful as the enchantress had promised. The merchant's business had prospered, and now the parents dressed their precious child in the finest silk that money could buy.

One day Sittukhan
was sitting on the
balcony, feeding her
canaries, when a handsome
young man came by on a horse.
'Who are you?' he asked.
'My name is Sittukhan,' replied the girl,
smiling behind her veil.

Just then the merchant's wife called from inside. 'Come in from the sun, my child.'

'I have to go,' said Sittukhan.

'I shall come past your house again next month,' said the young man. 'Promise me you will be here, waiting for me.'

'I promise,' said Sittukhan.

But the next morning she was again feeding her canaries when an old beggar knocked on the door to ask her mother for water. 'Why does your daughter waste her time looking after birds?' said the old crone. 'All girls her age should be embroidering cotton sheets for their wedding chest. Why don't you send her to the seamstress who'll teach her to sew?'

Sittukhan overheard the conversation.
'What is cotton?' she asked her mother.
'Why have I never seen it or even heard
of it? And why do I not learn to sew like
other girls?'

The merchant's wife had no choice but to
tell her daughter all about the witch's
curse and why she had removed
every scrap of cotton from
the house.

Sittukhan did
not believe her.

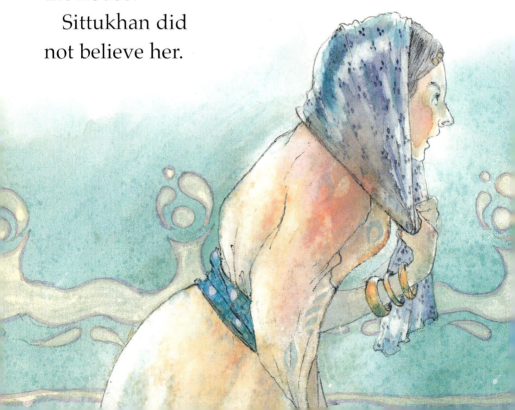

'Pah! How could touching a piece of cloth kill you?' she laughed. 'The idiocies old people believe in!'

And after lunch, when her mother had fallen asleep, she slipped out of the house and asked the way to the seamstress's workshop. She drew her silk cloak around her and hurried through the streets.

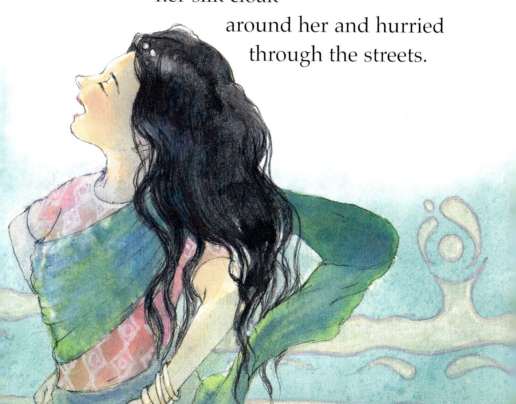

At the workshop, Sittụkhan sat on the
floor with the other pupils and watched the
seamstress work. How the needle seemed to
fly in her expert hands, diving in and out of
the material faster than the eye could see.

When the seamstress held up a robe she
was sewing for a caliph, everyone gasped.
It was embroidered all over with fish and

doves, and canaries just like the ones
Sittukhan had on her balcony.

'They look almost real,' said Sittukhan
and, before she knew it, she'd reached out
to stroke a canary. Alas, the moment
Sittukhan touched the cotton thread, the
world grew dark around her. Just as the
witch had predicted, she fell down dead!

Her mother and father were inconsolable. They refused to bury their beloved daughter under the ground. Instead they built her a glass palace, in the middle of a secret lake far from their city. There they laid her to rest on an ivory bed, in a chamber with her  favourite poems written in gold high on the walls. All around the palace they planted a garden, full of herbs and perfumed trees.

Now it so happened that the young man who had spoken to Sittukhan was a prince. When he passed by her house again a month later and found her not there, he was heartbroken. He instructed his wazir to find out where she had gone. The servant asked around the city and told his master all he heard. 'Sire, she lies dead in a glass palace, in the middle of a secret lake far away.'

The two men found the lake and rowed
out to the palace. As he approached the
door to Sittukhan's chamber, the prince said
to the wazir, 'Wait out here for me while I
pay my last respects. I shall not be long.'

He went in alone, and knelt by the bed.
How beautiful Sittukhan looked in her
silken robes. Her skin was still glowing, her
hair still shone. The prince took her hand
and kissed it over and over again.

'My beloved,' he sobbed.
'If only I had taken you
away with me the first
time I saw you, none
of this would have
happened.'

The prince was about to kiss Sittukhan's hand again when he noticed a fragment of cotton caught behind the nail on her thumb. It had got stuck there when Sittukhan touched the caliph's cloak. Gently, he drew it out.

All at once Sittukhan let out a sigh and opened her eyes. 'Where am I?' she whispered.

'You are with me,' said the prince. He kissed Sittukhan on the lips and she kissed him back. The two of them stayed there, gazing into each other's eyes, for forty days and forty nights. At last the prince stirred and said, 'My wazir must be getting hungry. I'll take him back to the palace and return for you with a golden litter.'

He left the chamber but, as he was
crossing the garden, he noticed a beautiful
rose swaying in the breeze.
'That flower reminds me of
Sittukhan's skin,' he said
to himself. And he
returned to the golden
room, where he admired
the velvety smoothness
of Sittukhan's skin for
another three days.

On the fourth day, he once again stood up and, promising Sittukhan he would return, left the room. This time he made it as far as the gate at the end of the garden. But, as he was opening the gate, a blackbird flew out of the bushes. 'That bird reminds me of Sittukhan's hair,' he said. And he returned to her once more, where he sat admiring the softness of her locks for another three days.

At last the wazir called out and said, 'Sire, they will be getting worried about us at the palace.'

'I am coming,' answered the prince. He kissed Sittukhan one last time and left the room.

'I wonder who he is talking to?' thought Sittukhan. And tiptoeing out of the chamber, she followed the prince down the marble steps into the garden.

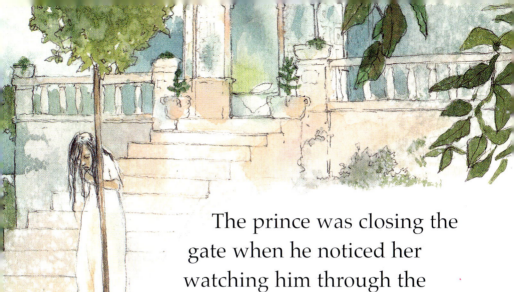

The prince was closing the gate when he noticed her watching him through the trees. 'You are not yet my wife,' he cried, 'but already you spy on me. You do not trust me, Sittukhan, and so I shall not return for you.' And he left without once looking back.

Halfway across the country the prince had a change of heart. How could I be so cruel to someone who loves me, he thought? And he turned back to fetch Sittukhan, but neither he nor the wazir, could find the secret lake again.

Meanwhile, Sittukhan wandered around the glass palace, sobbing with grief. How could someone who swore he loved her leave her for such a small mistake? 'I wasn't spying on him,' she cried. 'I only wanted to know who his friend was. Oh, I wish I was really dead.'

She was about to throw herself in the lake when she noticed something sparkling in the water. It was a golden ring, with a scarlet diamond on top. Sittukhan rubbed it against her arm to clean it.

In a flash of red smoke, a genie appeared in front of her. 'Speak, mortal,' he bellowed. 'Your wish is my command.'

'I desire a marble palace right next to that of the prince,' said Sittukhan.

'Shut your eyes,' ordered the genie.

Sittukhan obeyed and, when she opened her eyes again, she was standing in a marble palace. She called for her servants and they put on her face a silken veil hung around with golden coins.

Sittukhan leaned out of the window and, some time later, saw the prince returning home on his horse. The prince looked up and saw her too. He had no idea who she was but her beautiful eyes reminded him of Sittukhan, whom he missed very much.

When he reached his palace, the prince
called for his mother. 'Take the young
woman next door a gift,' he commanded.
'I want to marry her.'

That very same afternoon, the queen
presented herself to Sittukhan and gave her
a priceless rug. 'My son sends you a gift as
a token of his love,' she said. 'Take it and
accept his hand in marriage.'

Sittukhan thanked the prince's mother, then called one of her servants. 'Tear this rag up into floor cloths,' she ordered.

The servant obeyed, cutting the rug into pieces right in front of the queen.

'The girl must be so rich, your gift was an insult to her,' said the prince when his mother returned home. 'Take her something better.'

The queen went back to Sittukhan's palace with a jade necklace.

Once again, Sittukhan accepted the gift but called her servant. 'Throw these peas to the pigeons,' she ordered.

When the queen saw the servant scattering the beads in the garden, she said, 'What will my son have to do to prove his love for you?'

Sittukhan answered, 'If he truly loves me, let him be wrapped in seven shrouds of white linen. Then carry him through the streets in a black litter. At night, bring him to my garden where my servants will bury him alive in a marble tomb.'

The queen said to
the prince, 'Forget her.
Her price is too terrible
to pay.'

'I have already lost one
beloved,' said the prince, 'I shall
not make the same mistake twice.'
And right there and then he fell to the
floor and closed his eyes as if he were
dead. His body was wrapped in seven
sheets of linen and carried on a litter
through the streets of the city. His mother
followed the funeral procession, tearing her
shawl and wailing.

At night the prince was set down in Sittukhan's garden, outside the marble tomb. When the mourners had left, Sittukhan came out dressed as one of her servants, with her veil drawn across her face. She unwrapped the sheets one by one until the prince was free.

'You must be very much in love with my mistress if you are willing to be buried alive for her,' she said.

'I am,' said the prince.

'But how long will your love last this time?' asked Sittukhan. 'How long will it be before she makes a small mistake and you throw her out?'

'I shall never leave her,' cried the prince. 'I have lost one I loved before and I never will again.'

'In that case,' said Sittukhan. 'I accept your hand in marriage.' And she removed her veil so that the prince might recognise her.

'It is you, my Sittukhan!' he cried. 'I shall never betray you again. I promise on my mother's heart.'

And he and Sittukhan remained there, gazing into each other's eyes for forty days and forty nights. And it is said that, when they got married, there was not a happier couple in all the world.

Sleeping Beauty

This version of Sleeping Beauty *was made famous by the brothers Grimm, who first published it in 1812. They called their story* Briar-rose, *the name of the sleeping princess. It appeared in their* Nursery and Household Tales, *a collection of folk stories the brothers had been told as they travelled around Germany.*

A long time ago there were a king and queen who had no children. But it happened that once, when the queen was bathing, a frog crept out of the water on to the land, and said to her, 'Your wish shall be fulfilled; soon you shall have a daughter.'
What the frog said came true and the queen had a little girl. The king could not contain himself for joy, and ordered a feast. He invited not only his relatives and friends, but also the wise women, so that they might give his child

magic gifts. There were thirteen of them in his kingdom, but, as he had only twelve golden plates, the eldest was left out.

At the feast the wise women bestowed their magic gifts upon the baby: one gave virtue, another beauty, a third riches, and so on, with everything in the world that she could wish for.

When eleven of them had made their promises, suddenly the thirteenth came in. She cried with a loud voice, 'The king's daughter shall in her fifteenth year prick herself with a spindle, and fall down dead.'

And, without saying a word more, she vanished.

Then the twelfth wise woman, whose good wish still remained unspoken, came forward and said, 'It shall not be death, but a deep sleep of a hundred years, into which the princess shall fall.'

The king, who was determined to keep his child safe, ordered every spindle in the kingdom to be burnt. Meanwhile the gifts of the wise women were fulfilled. The princess grew up to be beautiful, modest, good-natured and wise.

Now it happened that on the day when she was fifteen years old, the king and queen were not at home, and the princess was left to play on her own. So she went round looking into rooms she had not been in before.

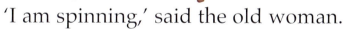

At last she came to an old tower. Climbing up the narrow, winding staircase and reaching a little door, she opened it to find an old woman spinning flax in a room.

'Good day,' said the princess. 'What are you doing?'

'I am spinning,' said the old woman.

'What sort of thing is that, rattling round so merrily?' asked the girl, and she reached out for the spindle.

Scarcely had she touched it when she pricked her finger with its pointed end. All at once she fell down upon a bed and lay there in a deep sleep.

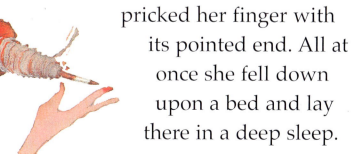

And this sleep extended over the whole
castle: the king and queen, who had just
come home, fell asleep and the whole of the
court with them. The horses, too, went to
sleep in the stable, the dogs in the yard, the
pigeons upon the roof, the flies on the wall;
even the fire that was flaming in the grate
became quiet and slept and the roast meat
left off frizzling. The cook,
who was reaching for
the scullery boy to
box his ears, went to
sleep. And the
wind fell, and on
the trees before the
castle not a leaf
moved again.

Round about the
castle there began to
grow a hedge of thorns,
which every year became higher and thicker

until it had covered it completely. But the story of the beautiful sleeping 'Briar-rose', for so the princess was named, went about the country, so that from time to time kings' sons came and tried to get through the thorny hedge into the castle.

They found it impossible, for the thorns held fast together, as if they had hands, and the youths were caught in them and died a miserable death.

After many years a king's son came again to that country, and heard an old man talking about the thorn-hedge, and that a castle was said to stand behind it in which a beautiful princess had been asleep for a hundred years.

By this time the hundred years had just passed, and the day had come when Briar-rose was to awake again. When the king's son came near to the thorn-hedge, it was nothing but large and beautiful flowers, which let him pass unhurt. In the castle he saw everyone and everything asleep, even the cook in the kitchen with his hand still out to seize the boy.

He went farther into the castle and came to the tower stairs. He climbed them and opened the door into the little room where Briar-rose was sleeping. There she lay, so beautiful that he could not turn his eyes away. He stooped down and gave her a kiss.

In that instant, Briar-rose awoke, and looked lovingly at the king's son. The two went down stairs together as the king and queen awoke and with them the whole court.

The horses in the stable stood up and shook themselves; the hounds jumped up; the pigeons upon the roof pulled out their heads from under their wings; the flies on the wall crept again; the fire in the kitchen burned up and flickered; the joint began to frizzle again; and the cook gave the boy such a box on the ear that he screamed.

And then the marriage of the king's son with Briar-rose was celebrated with all splendour, and they lived contented to the end of their days.

Taking it further

Once you've read both stories in this book, there is lots more you can think and talk about. There's plenty to write about, too.

• For starters, think about what is the same and what is different about the two stories. Talk about these with other people. Which story do you prefer and why?

• Imagine you were organising a christening or a naming ceremony for a relative. Make a detailed guest list. Who would you invite to the feast and who would you leave out? Why?

• Rewrite one of the stories in a modern setting, perhaps placing yourself in the main role. How would your plot differ from the old ones, and why? Would your princess behave in the same way as Sittukhan or Briar-rose?

• Draw up plans for Sittukhan's and Briar-rose's palaces. How would they be different? You need to think about the materials used, the furniture, decorations and even the garden design.